Bed Time for Little Bear

By Katrina Donahue

Bed Time for Little Bear by Katrina Donahue

Published by Shiny Chicken Studios
PO Box 711404 Santee, CA 92072

ISBN: 978-0-578-95206-2

For Jasper,
my own little bear.

It's time for bed
little bear.

You've brushed your teeth.

You've combed your hair.

Read stories in our rocking chair.

It's time for little bears
to sleep.

Mommy!
What's that?

That's the wind going
whoosh, whoosh, whoosh.

Hush now little one,
it's time for little bears
to sleep.

Mommy!
What's that?

That's the rain going
pat, pat, pat.

Hush now silly one,
it's time for little bears
to sleep.

Mommy!
What's that?

That's the chair going
creak, creak, creak.

Hush now precious one,
it's time for little bears
to sleep.

Mommy!
What's that?

That's the cat going
purr, purr, purr.

Hush now snuggly one,
it's time for little bears
to sleep.

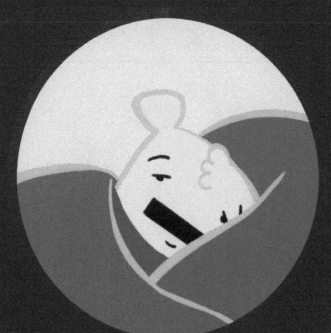

Little bear's eyes
are getting heavy.

Quiet snores
fill the air.

"What's that?"
Mommy whispers.

"That's my little bear
fast asleep."

Good night little bear.

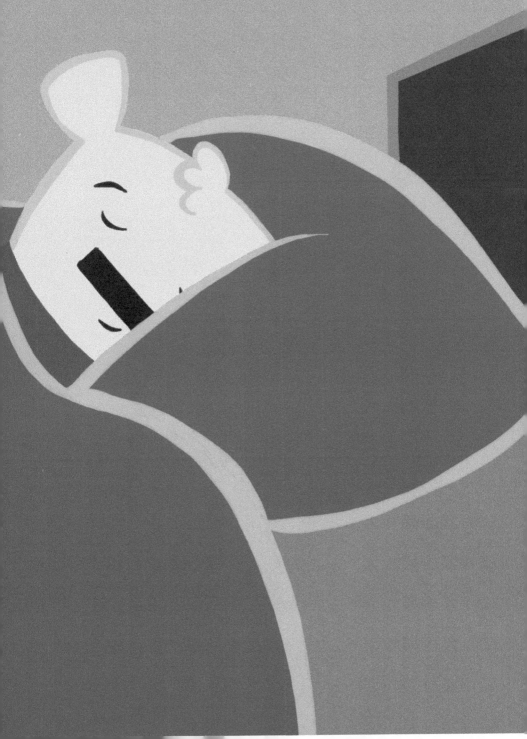

CPSIA information can be obtained
at www.ICGtesting.com
Printed in the USA
LVHW070123280721
693914LV00004B/155